The Mermaid of Warsaw

and other tales from Poland

Richard Monte

Illustrated by Paul Hess

F

FRANCES LINCOLN
CHILDREN'S BOOKS

Contents

Introduction

In the heart of Warsaw's majestic Old Town sits the statue of a mermaid. Tourists flock to take photos of the statue in summer. I have been among them, wandering through the cobbled streets admiring the beautiful pink, blue and yellow houses so characteristic of Polish cities.

But go to the Warsaw History Museum in the Old Town Square, and a different story unfolds. For inside this building are black and white photographs dating from the Second World War. The Royal Castle with its orange walls, the yellow façade of St John's Cathedral, those lovely coloured houses and medieval churches – are all reduced to rubble.

Now look out of the museum window, and, like magic, you'll see the Old Town restored to life again. Soon after the end of the war, the whole of Warsaw's historic heart was re-created using the eighteenth-century paintings of Bernardo Bellotto, nephew of the renowned landscape painter Canaletto. This miraculous act of conservation is typical of the Polish spirit. Like Poland's two mermaids (the original sits by the bank of the River Vistula), the Polish people stubbornly refuse to give in, no matter what misfortune befalls them.

The other tales in this book are just as bewitching as 'The Mermaid of Warsaw'. I hope they will give you a glimpse of some less well known regions of the country, and if you happen to travel there, you might see just how powerful folk tales can be. For example, in Poznan, each day at noon, a pair of silver goats emerge from a door above the clock on the Renaissance town hall and butt their heads together twelve times. It is rumoured that if you stay in the Wieliczka salt mine at night, you might see a ghost! Tales about the phantom underground Treasurer are rife – and that's not surprising, for he's lived there long enough. The mine has been in continuous operation since the thirteenth century.

Stray into the mysterious mountains of Karkonosze and you might find an old, crumbling castle where a wizened little man sits counting turnips all day long. You can sail on one of the Polish lakes where the shadows of kings and fish lurk beneath the surface. If you visit the Baltic Coast, don't linger too long, for if you do, the vision of a city drifting out at sea might tempt you to catch a boat to a place where the citizens harbour a terrible secret...

Or you can stay in Warsaw, sit by the mermaid, and wait. As dusk falls, her haunting song will take you back to the time when this great city was little more than a fishing hamlet perched on the river bank.

The Goats of Poznan

The Mayor of Poznan, a plump and self-important-looking man with a curly black moustache, was standing in the centre of the medieval marketplace, staring up in wonder at the Town Hall. It really was a pearl.

"Splendid! Splendid!" he muttered to himself. Its formal architecture perfectly crowned the jumble of timber and brick buildings which made up the square. Admiring the painted frieze of Jagiellonian kings, the Mayor congratulated himself on his decision to build the Town Hall in this style. It was so much more impressive than the Gothic building it had replaced following a fire. He surveyed the flag covering the wall below the frieze and beamed with pride. The jewel in the crown lay behind the flag and soon it would be unveiled for everyone to see.

The Mayor clicked his fingers. Punctuality! That's what it was all about – a rich and prosperous town which ran like clockwork. Soon, everyone would know the time and no one would be late for work, or school, or church again! And he congratulated himself on the great feast he had arranged for the Governor of Wielkopolska to celebrate the official opening of the clock. He could sit back and relax knowing that Mr Goose, the greatest chef in Poznan, was in charge of the food.

Fat, bumbling, pompous old Mr Goose, with red cheeks the size of melons and a belly that had digested far more than its fair share of hams, sausages, dumplings and sweet poppy-seed buns and jam doughnuts, saw this as his chance to establish himself as the greatest cook in Poland.

A yellow lamp shone in the kitchen of "The Goose", an old, timber-framed inn standing at the corner of a cobbled street off the main town square.

It was the night before the big day

and old Mr Goose, humming to himself, checked that everything in the oak-beamed kitchen was ready. The work surfaces were spotless, the oven trays sparkling, the spit clean and the fire stoked with logs and coals.

"Goose, you're a genius. Play this one right, and the whole country'll be talking about you." And picking up a small glass of vodka, he toasted his good fortune, "*Na zdrowie!*" Then, with a warm, lighthearted feeling creeping through his body, he made his way through the dining-room, past the round wooden tables already set with gold-rimmed menus. Mr Goose licked his lips in anticipation as he caught sight of the main meal described on the cards:

Wild Boar
spit-roast over an open fire
with tender forest mushrooms
and a selection
of the finest
garden vegetables

He could almost smell the crackling and dripping fat. The Governor loved roast boar: it was his favourite dish. And Goose was going to serve him the best boar he'd ever tasted in his life.

With that thought, he tiptoed up the wooden stairway to his room, pausing outside the bedroom of his young apprentice to make sure all was quiet. The young lad had a big day ahead of him and he was going to need all the sleep he could get!

Things seemed quiet enough. What Mr Goose did not realise was that Pietrek, his young apprentice, who had been scrubbing the kitchen from floor to ceiling, was still wide awake.

As Pietrek lay in his hard wooden bed, the threadbare blanket pulled up to his chin and his wide eyes peeping out over the covers, he couldn't stop thinking how hard life seemed, and how tiring it was working for a master who never gave him a moment's peace. Mr Goose had done nothing but fuss and fret about the Governor's visit – and it was Pietrek who had done all the hard work. It was all too much for a boy – and he was lying there with all the cares in the world on his young shoulders, not getting a wink of sleep…

The next thing the young apprentice heard was a loud rap on his door and a voice booming out into the morning like a bull.

"Pietrek! Get up, lad! We've got work to do!"

And what a morning it proved to be. Goose, the old tyrant, didn't give Pietrek a moment to catch his breath. His orders echoed around the inn.

"Polish the plates!"

"Lay the tables!"

"Chop the vegetables!"

"Turn the spit!"

Poor Pietrek. He didn't even have time to snatch a slice of bread for his breakfast, and now old Goose, puffed up and pleased as punch, as if he'd done all the work himself, decided to leave the young lad in charge while he nipped out into the square to listen to the fireman's band which was just striking up a tune.

"Pietrek, the brass are playing. You know how much I love brass, lad. I'll be gone ten minutes. Ten minutes, that's all. Just sit here quietly and turn the spit. My, that boar's starting to smell good. Don't do anything silly, now…"

And with that he was gone, disappearing into the crowds gathering in the square to listen to the music, relaxed and smiling, knowing that everything was under control. Soon the Governor would be sitting down to the most delicious meal he'd ever had in his life.

Pietrek sighed, and stared at the roasting boar as he turned the spit. The skin was beginning to turn a beautiful golden-yellow colour, and the smell was making his mouth water. Goodness me, he felt hungry. He could hear his stomach rumbling like a bass drum and he had to keep shifting his position to stop the noise. If only he could sneak a slice of bread to ease this raging hunger! Old Goose had said he'd be gone for ten minutes. It would take less than a couple of minutes to get to the bread bin and back. He could wolf down a slice in no time.

Without a further thought, Pietrek let go of the spit and dashed for the parlour. A honey-brown cottage loaf had already been cut ready for the guests. Mr Goose wouldn't know how many slices there were, surely. It was too tempting.

Pietrek reached out and snatched one, but before it reached his mouth he heard a crash, followed by a strange sizzling sound.

Oh no – the roast! He dropped the bread and dashed back into the kitchen.

What a scene greeted his eyes! The roast boar – the golden-yellow, sweet-smelling pride and joy that Mr Goose had been talking about for days, the wild roast boar cooked to impress Governor Wojewoda, had slipped off the spit into the flames and was beginning to turn black!

The young apprentice picked up a poker and started prodding about in desperation. Smoke was pouring into his eyes and filling the kitchen. Tears were streaming down his face. Old Goose would kill him! He almost wished it was him and not the boar burning on that fire.

Mr Goose waddled round the corner, tapping the air with his fists and humming the tune he had heard. Brass! How he loved it! But as the inn came into view, he was met with an unwelcome sight. Black smoke was pouring out of the kitchen window.

Old Goose's heart missed a beat. He lurched forward, almost tripping on the cobblestones and sending himself flying. One thought, and one thought alone was on his mind: THE ROAST BOAR!

Imagine his horror when he hurled himself through the kitchen door and saw the fire greedily devouring the remains of the roast! Enraged, he grabbed hold of Pietrek and twisted his ears, ignoring the snivelling apprentice's tears and wailing.

"You've carbonised the boar! I'll give you a thrashing for this! What the devil am I going to serve the Governor now? Oh, my reputation! My reputation!"

Goose's cheeks were purple and steam was coming out of his nose. He shook the young lad so violently, Pietrek's shirt ripped at the seams.

"I'll see to it that you never work again – for me or anyone else. Now, get out! Go and buy me some new meat, while I sort out this mess. Now! This minute! And make sure it's tender. Get out!" And he kicked the apprentice through the door.

Pietrek left as fast as he could, rubbing his sore backside, mumbling how sorry he was, and relieved to be away from the inn and its furious proprietor. The young lad knew the narrow, cobbled streets of Poznan like an old friend, but that didn't prevent him tripping up twice in his haste to get to the butcher. Out of the corner of his eye he noticed that both the bakery and the shoemaker's were closed; their doors were shut tight and their blinds pulled down. Everyone was in the square.

Pietrek stopped to catch his breath, worried that the butcher might also have closed for the day in order to enjoy the celebrations. He found himself standing outside a cottage with a red wooden door. It was known locally as the House of the Argumentative Widow. A window was open on the ground floor and a high-pitched woman's voice, screeching like an angry bird, reached Pietrek out in the street.

"Marta! You're not going to any celebrations until you've scrubbed this floor properly. I want to see it sparkle! Then get yourself cleaned up, girl. My snow-white darlings look better than you!"

Pietrek knew poor Marta, the girl who had taken a job as a cleaner at the House of the Argumentative Widow, but he wasn't thinking of her now. He was staring at a pair of beautiful white goats which were tied to the garden gate by a thin rope.

Well, what a bit of luck! Convincing himself that the butcher must be closed by now, Pietrek carefully opened the garden gate and untied the rope. These two would make a delicious roast. He just hoped that Governor Wojewoda liked goat!

He could still hear the voice of the Argumentative Widow berating her cleaner, but without further thought the young lad started back along the cobbled streets with the animals.

"Come on! No, this way! That's it. No, stop eating those flowers!"

My goodness, those goats were stubborn! All the

way back they pulled and strained this way and that. By the time Pietrek reached the inn, he was hot, sweaty and felt as if he'd been dragged through a bush backwards. But his troubles had only just begun. The two goats, separated from their mistress, instinctively realised that this was not where they lived, and started throwing themselves around wildly, snapping the thin rope that held them.

"Hey! Come back!" shouted Pietrek desperately, but the two goats scampered off in the direction of the square, which by now was heaving with loud music, dancing and singing.

A little boy broke away from the crowd and started chasing the goats, closely pursued by the Argumentative Widow, who was shrieking wildly and waving her fists.

"My goats! My darlings! Someone help me!"

Everyone, including Pietrek, turned to see the widow lurch forward just as the goats slipped into the doorway of the County Hall! But no one liked the old woman, and her pleas fell on deaf ears.

"Look, that's him over there! That wretched boy stole my goats!"

Pietrek put his head in his hands. What was he going to do now? Suddenly the clock started chiming midday. The Governor's carriage had arrived and the Mayor was waiting eagerly to show him the wonderful new clock. The flag fluttered in the breeze as the drum roll boomed out.

Governor Wojewoda tipped his head back and squinted.

"Well, I'll be damned. They've got goats up there! Look at them butting their horns!"

Before anyone could do or say anything, the Argumentative Widow leapt forward.

"Those are *my* goats! In the tower, sir! That little good-for-nothing thief!"

Governor Wojewoda looked at the woman.

"What thief? A thief locked in the tower?" And turning to the people, he announced: "Those goats must be returned to their rightful owner and the thief must be prosecuted! Now, come on, who stole them? Own up!"

A little voice spoke up. "It was me, sir."

Governor Wojewoda looked down at Pietrek, whose knees were knocking with fear. The crowd leered at the boy, as the scowling Mayor and Old Goose fumed angrily over him.

"Goats, eh? Are you telling me that you've got time to play with goats?" cried Goose, purple-faced.

But he didn't have time to say anything else, for the Governor said, "Let the lad tell his story."

Everyone listened as Pietrek explained how he'd

burnt the roast, and how his master had sent him out to the butcher. Mr Goose shuffled uncomfortably in his shoes as the crowd looked disapprovingly at him.

Things were now clear. Governor Wojewoda raised his hand.

"Well, by right you deserve a damn good hiding, but on this day of celebration, to make amends for your misdemeanour you will help the master clockmaker carve two identical white goats in wood. These will be installed in the tower to commemorate the occasion. On the chime of twelve each day, they will butt each other's horns. Now, go and collect your goats, old widow."

And turning to Mr Goose, he added, "I will be satisfied with chicken broth. I am sure, Mr Goose, you have a chicken or two at the ready."

Mr Goose blushed, "Oh of course, sir, chicken! What a splendid idea!" And grabbing Pietrek by the collar, he dragged him back to the inn to prepare the meal.

Now, even young Pietrek couldn't spoil chicken broth... could he?

The Mermaid of Warsaw

The red glow of the hot summer sun had vanished and a full moon hung over the little fishing hamlet. A young fisherman whose name was Stanislaw leaned out of his window watching the yellow stars twinkling in the black sky and listening to the gentle lapping of the River Vistula. A breeze hummed through the darkness.

Suddenly his ear picked up a thin metallic sound, a delicate tinkling like a silver bell singing in the night.

Stanislaw climbed into his little wooden bed. All through the night he tossed and turned, his head full of the faint melody ringing softly on the air. Finally he slept – he had to be up early in the morning to fetch salt from the castle.

"It was a tinny sound. The wind wouldn't make a noise like that," thought Stanislaw, as he packed his crate into the fish cart and set off to meet his friends who were also taking their wares to the Castle of the Mazovian Princes.

Stanislaw and Szymon sat in the cart, while Mateusz rode a brown stallion.

As they travelled north through the dense oak and larch forests, the three fishermen exchanged stories.

"I couldn't sleep a wink, either! It didn't sound like a silver bell to me, though, Stach. It was a haunting melody – a violin crying and laughing through the night," said Szymon, rubbing his bobbly nose.

"More like a lark singing of love under the moon, Szymon. At least, that's what it sounded like to me," added Mateusz, with the freckled face.

They had come to the end of the forest. Ahead of them, perched majestically on a grassy peak, was the stone castle. The three friends drove up to the iron gates. Three crates of freshly caught fish from the Vistula went into the hands of the gatekeeper, and in return three large cloth bags full of Wieliczka salt were handed over to the fishermen.

"Good health to you, sir. And please, don't forget to pass on our respects and wishes to the wise princes," they called out to him.

They rode back in silence. All three had the same thing on their minds. At last, Szymon spoke.

"We ought to be thankful for this trade with Mazovia."

"Thankful yes – but not complacent," declared Mateusz, turning his head. "Fish is fine, as far as it goes, but there are more desirable things in this world."

"You're right, Mateusz. But it is not for us simple fishermen to pry into mysterious sounds," muttered Stanislaw.

"You worry too much, Stach… but now I think of it, princes love novelty. What would they give us if we could find the source of this ethereal music?" asked Szymon, his eyes glinting as he spoke.

They rode on until the oak trees folded over their heads and blacked out the blue sky. By the time they reached the hamlet, they were hatching a cunning plan. They discussed it as they sat on the green banks of the river, eating their freshly buttered bread and drinking frothy goat's milk.

"It would be easier to wait for the full moon to come around again," mused Szymon.

"You're right. Under the full moon we'd have plenty of light to see what's going on," observed Mateusz.

Stanislaw chewed on a fresh crust and rolled his eyes. "We can't wait for another full moon. We don't know how long this singing will continue. I say we go this evening. We could finish early and get back in time to hide in the bushes over there before the sun begins to set." He pointed to a cluster of reeds growing by the bank.

Reluctantly the others agreed with Stanislaw's plan. They didn't want to appear frightened in the eyes of their bold young friend.

✳ ✳ ✳

The yellow bush of reeds which grew on the marshy banks of the Vistula was tall and dense enough to hide the three fishermen as they crouched in the middle. As the orange sun began to redden, Stanislaw crept forward and gently parted the reeds.

"See anything yet, Stach?" hissed Szymon.

"Keep your voice down," said Mateusz.

Stanislaw, who was the smallest of the three, was almost at the edge of the water, when all at once the sun turned into a red ball and once more the air was filled with an enchanting sound. The tinkling silver bell was drawing him towards the water. The other two were following behind, consumed by the angelic sounds of a violin and a lark.

Stanislaw reached the edge of the reeds. And there, beneath the glowing red orb of the sun, was the loveliest creature he had ever seen: a woman with golden hair flowing down her back in a waterfall, with eyes as deep as the blue sea, and a slender curving body covered in turquoise scales like an exotic fish.

Soon they all saw her, and they stood rooted to the ground unable to move while those beautiful sounds of bells, larks and violins filled the night air. And there they stayed, while the blood-red sun slipped over the horizon, excited and a bit scared by their wonderful discovery. At last, when the sky finally darkened, the singing stopped and the mermaid vanished. None of them could remember the exact moment when she slipped below the surface of the water.

For the rest of the evening the three fishermen couldn't think of anything else, and after a sleepless night filled with dreams of the sublime creature they'd seen, they gathered in Stanislaw's kitchen.

"We must find out who she is," cried Szymon.

"If we could only catch her, my friend, imagine what those princes would pay for her!" exclaimed Mateusz.

"Listen, both of you. Before we attempt to capture this creature, we ought to consult Father Barnaba. He will know what to do, mark my words," said Stanislaw.

Wise old Father Barnaba, thin as a bean-pole, with a snow-white beard and a bald head, lived the life of a hermit in a ramshackle hut in the depths of the forest. He was just finishing his prayers when the three fishermen arrived. They caught sight of his brown, shapeless, fraying bag of a habit approaching the narrow window and then his familiar face, wrinkled with wisdom, beamed out and smiled.

"Good afternoon, dear brothers. What brings you so deep into the forest?"

Stanislaw hesitated, while his two friends bit their lips nervously.

"We… we've come to ask for your advice," they blurted out.

Father Barnaba winked, his bushy white eyebrows dancing up and down on his shiny forehead.

"Let me see. Three fishermen in the forest. Three nervous-looking fishermen. This can only mean one thing. Someone's been disturbing the fish!" he observed knowingly.

Szymon's chestnut eyes sparkled.

"Well, in a way you are right, Father. We've seen a heavenly mermaid in the river, and when she sings, none of us can sleep a wink. The music makes our souls leap for joy."

"Well, I've heard some things in my time, but this beats them all!" exclaimed the hermit. "Tell me, when does this usually happen?"

"She sings through the night when there is a full moon. At other times, she starts at sunset and stops when the sun has disappeared beneath the horizon," recalled Mateusz.

"What is this singing like, exactly?" enquired Father Barnaba.

"It's impossible to describe! And the funny thing is, we all hear her music differently. It reminds me of a silver bell. Szymon here speaks of a lark singing, and Mateusz thinks he hears a violin!" exclaimed Stanislaw.

"Well, my good men. What do you want an old

man like me to do about it? It sounds as if you three are having a wonderful time!" said Father Barnaba.

"Oh, no, Father, don't get us wrong. It's remarkable to think there is a real mermaid in our river, but the sound leaves us tossing and turning at night. It's affected our fishing! And all this has made Mateusz's and Szymon's wives extremely cross!" cried Stanislaw.

"Wives! Ah... now I understand everything! Don't think that just because I haven't got one myself, I can't appreciate your problem. If one of your good ladies were to find out that you'd been cavorting with a mermaid, there'd be trouble. There's nothing for it – you'll have to get rid of the creature, quick!"

"How, Father? Please tell us how!" implored Szymon.

"Come inside for a moment," whispered Father Barnaba mysteriously.

They seated themselves on oak-log stools at a round table. The hermit leaned forward, coughed and began.

"Now let's see, what have we got? You say that this mermaid only sings through the night under a full moon."

"Yes, that's right, Father," the three of them chimed back.

"Good. A full moon it has to be, then. You'll need time. And light. Plenty of it. You'll also need a good, sturdy boat and a strong net. Although I doubt whether that'll pose you three a problem!" he said, chuckling to himself.

The three fishermen listened intently.

"Now, let's see. A boat. A net. What else? Ah yes – the branches and leaves of a lime tree. You'll need to disguise yourselves. Go to the mermaid dressed as trees, smelling of lime. You mustn't smell human, or she'll run a mile!"

Szymon clapped his hands.

"Is that it, Father? Splendid! And just think what the Mazovian Princes will pay for a mermaid!"

Father Barnaba winked, and the eager fishermen got up to leave.

"Just one more thing!" the old hermit called out.

The three friends stopped in their tracks.

"Remember to put wax in your ears when you do this. If you hear that weeping and wailing sound when you catch her, it'll be game over. She'll have all three of you hypnotised in no time, and you'll feel so much pity for her, none of you will be able to catch her. Then there'll be no bag of gold waiting for you in Mazovia Castle. And don't think it will be easy. Mermaids are beautiful on the surface, but inside, some of them can be as cunning and spiteful as witches!" Father Barnaba's words echoed around the room.

***

Szymon, Mateusz and Stanislaw waited eagerly for the next full moon, preparing themselves just as the wise hermit had advised. The boat and net were soon ready, and on the appointed night they crept down to the bank, their heads and arms covered in bushy leaves and branches. There was a strong scent of lime in the air as they approached the river. Little clusters of white and red peonies shone under the soft yellow light of the moon.

The three fishermen, their ears plugged with wax, crept towards the bank, took up their positions among the rushes and settled down patiently to wait – looking for all the world like three strange trees growing among the reeds. Szymon kept tugging nervously at his corner of the fishing net, peering out for any sign of the elusive mermaid. Time stood still, and their little boat bobbed about at the water's edge.

Then, just when they had almost lost patience, the ethereal creature appeared. Once again, she was the most beautiful vision they had ever seen upon the Earth! Long, blonde hair decorated with water lilies curled down her graceful back, and her dark blue eyes were as radiant as a glimmering sea.

Quick as a flash, the three fishermen hurled the net out on to the water and watched it fall down over their prey. The bewildered mermaid struggled to free herself, but the more she turned, the more entangled she became. Jumping out and throwing off their disguises, the three fishermen were soon in the boat and rowing furiously towards the writhing mermaid. It wasn't easy getting her in the vessel. She was crying and wailing all the while, and they thanked Father Barnaba for his gift of wax.

They hoisted her up on a cart and pulled it into the village. Stanislaw held the rickety wooden door of his old barn open, while the other two dragged their prisoner inside. Then Szymon and Mateusz waved goodbye to their young friend. He was to keep watch while they fetched a more sumptuous carriage to take their catch to the Mazovian Castle at dawn light.

But do you think it is easy being locked up near a creature so exotic, so alluring, so exquisitely beautiful? Poor Stanislaw sat and watched as the mermaid wriggled and writhed, twisting her curvaceous body into knots, tears streaming down her sad face. He watched her lips moving and fell into a trance, wondering what on earth this wonderful creature was saying. Suddenly it was all too much for him. Without even realising what he was doing, he pulled out his ear wax.

Suddenly the room was filled with pitiful cries, and at the sound of that lilting voice, Stanislaw fell into a trance. He would do anything for this sublime creature. Anything!

"Free me from the shackles of this horrible net! Let me go back to the river where I belong! I beg you! Please let me go!" the beautiful voice cried.

Soon the young man was wrestling with the knots which bound the net, cutting at them eagerly with a knife, laughing as the hole grew bigger, until finally the mermaid jumped through and was free.

How quickly she could hop on that tail of hers, out through the barn door and back down to the river, with the little fisherman skipping behind her like a lovesick fool!

When Szymon and Mateusz returned to find the barn door swinging on its rusty hinges, they thought something terrible had happened to their friend. Once inside, they were dismayed to find the torn fishing net lying on the hay bales, but of Stanislaw there was no sign.

"We shouldn't have left him alone," began Szymon – then, realising that his friend couldn't hear him, he pulled out the wax plugs.

"I said, we shouldn't have left him alone with the creature!"

Mateusz looked annoyed.

"There's no need to shout!" he countered, surveying the ground.

"Look, Szymon. Flipper marks. They went this way – back towards the river!"

That was when they heard the mermaid's voice again – and this time she sounded angry. Her spell was broken.

All Szymon and Mateusz could think about now was rescuing their friend.

"Stach! Leave her! Let her go!" they shouted

as they approached the river bank. But Stanislaw couldn't hear them. He was staring into the mermaid's sea-blue eyes.

All at once he hurled himself into the water. There was an almighty splash and he disappeared, resurfacing a moment later at the side of the beautiful creature. Much to his friends' horror, she curled her fins around the young fisherman.

"Give him back!" they shouted.

"Never!" sang the mermaid. "You tried to catch me as if I was a mere fish. You wanted to keep me as your prisoner on the land. You wanted to make me sing. I was here to tell you that your little fishing hamlet will one day grow into a great and prosperous city. But now I am returning to the sea, and I shall take your friend with me."

"You can't do that! You can't take Stach. He's got his whole life ahead of him…"

Their words disappeared into thin air. The mermaid had gone, taking Stanislaw with her.

A great sadness fell upon the two fishermen and as they turned dejectedly towards home, they heard a voice on the wind.

"One day, when this hamlet is a thriving city I will come back and protect its people from danger, for I carry with me a sword and a shield."

Szymon and Mateusz didn't know what to think. But they never forgot what had happened, and told everyone about their meeting with the entrancing creature.

Many years later, the good people of Warsaw built a statue of the mermaid in the centre of their city. You see, if she ever does come back, they want her to feel truly at home!

Skarbnik's Second Breakfast

Salt!

Desire for the precious green mineral kept the miners of Wieliczka wide awake at night. How many times had one of them dreamt of discovering it and leapt out of bed shouting, "Eureka!" – only to wake up and find that he hadn't discovered anything…

***

The moon was up, and deep underground Szymon was still crawling along the dark, damp tunnels of the salt mine, a tallow lamp in one hand.

When he got home from the mine that evening, he was in unusually high spirits. He might not have found his vein of precious salt, but at the foot of a knobbly stalagmite he *had* come face to face with

Skarbnik the Treasurer! They had stared at each other for a second or two before Skarbnik turned and vanished.

Everyone at the mine knew about Skarbnik, an underground spirit who puffed away on a pipe and was said to reward the good and punish the bad. Nervous miners whispered about the dangers of angering him and often left small offerings at the side of passages: slices of spicy sausage, crusts of bread, pieces of carrot, then wished their ghostly guardian good health and hurried on, pickaxe in hand.

Skarbnik's long white beard and deeply furrowed face remained in Szymon's head long after their strange encounter. At supper that evening, you could have cut the silence with a knife. Eventually Szymonowa, his wife, asked her usual question: "Did anything happen at work today, husband?"

The old miner had no choice but to tell her.

"Yes… um…" he stammered. "You may think I'm mad… but… I spoke to an apparition… a ghost… He's known as the Treasurer… the Keeper of the Mine…"

His wife burst out laughing.

"Well, really, Szymon! Do you expect me to believe such nonsense? A ghost, indeed! I think you need a good night's sleep!"

***

Now, quite apart from salt, Szymon had another passion, and that was playing cards. Everyone in Wieliczka knew of his devilish skill at card games. He had never lost a round – poker, bridge, pontoon, rummy, you name it, there wasn't a miner in the place who could beat him. They would wink at him and tease him, saying, "You know what they say, Szymon: lucky at cards, unlucky in love!"

"Ha, ha. Very funny. I've already got a wife, so it makes no difference to me!"

Now, everything got back sooner or later to Skarbnik, so it wasn't long before the old ghost heard about Szymon's extraordinary success at the card table. And let me tell you, Skarbnik wasn't happy about it, for he liked to think of himself as the greatest player underground.

"Who is this little man trying to compete with me?" he said irritably.

One week later, Szymon came face to face with the guardian of the mine again. This time, he felt a bit faint. His knees began to quake as he tried desperately to remember the last time he'd left a morsel out for Skarbnik. He tried to recall how he'd been behaving recently. "Am I dishonest? Do I argue?" he wondered.

"Have I hurt anyone? Do I use bad language?"

Sweating and trembling, he stared hard at the ground and waited a moment – which seemed to last a thousand years – for Skarbnik to speak.

"Well Szymon, fancy a game of cards with me?" rumbled the ghost.

The petrified miner's hands were shaking so badly, his pickaxe nearly fell out of his hand.

"I have a little proposition for you," went on the ghost. "Beat me at cards, and I will give you what you most desire…"

Szymon looked up hopefully, wondering how much salt he could win within a couple of hours…

"And if I lose?" he asked.

"Lose? You, Szymon, the man who can beat anyone at cards, lose? It's unlikely, isn't it? But if that were to happen, if by chance I beat you, then all I ask is that you bring me my second breakfast."

"Second breakfast!" exclaimed Szymon, as if to say, *Is that all?*

"That's right, my second breakfast – let's say, a piece of bread and butter. What do you say?"

Szymon agreed. For one thing, he didn't intend to lose. For another, if he lost, then his wife could surely give him an extra sandwich in the morning. And lastly, he reckoned that when he won, he could sit back while old Skarbnik did all his dirty work in the mine!

"Perfect. When do we start?" asked Szymon.

"Tomorrow. I'll meet you in the mine when the time is right. And don't worry about cards. I've got a brand new pack."

✳ ✳ ✳

The wavering shadow of Szymon's lighted candle flickered as he crept along the narrow passages of the mine. He had strayed far away from the heavily worked tunnels, for it was here that he had agreed to meet Skarbnik.

He waited patiently, listening to the steady drip-drip of a dangling stalactite, and peered into an icy pool of salt water on the ground. Szymon tried to visualise the magnificent underground salt palace where the Treasurer was rumoured to live, according to centuries-old stories told by the miners. He imagined ornate chandeliers carved from salt and shimmering doors studded with delicate crystals... so he hardly noticed when Skarbnik suddenly appeared out of the opposite wall.

Szymon pinched himself to check he wasn't dreaming, and followed the underground lord in silence along a narrow corridor of stone. Gigantic walls of rock seemed to open up as the Treasurer took his friend deeper within the ground.

Eventually they reached the outskirts of the great palace, and Szymon gasped in awe as he looked at the beautiful spires and minarets stretching up towards the roof of the mine.

They stopped suddenly before a small porch. Skarbnik pushed open a heavy oak door. Inside was a room which smelt of tobacco, with a great, round, carved table in the middle. Skarbnik puffed at his pipe and a ring of white smoke wafted into the air.

"This is my card room. Come in, my good man. Let's play!" he growled.

Skarbnik soon realised how experienced his opponent was. No matter what they played – poker, rummy, bridge – Szymon was always one step ahead. – the Treasurer lost the lot. When they were playing their final game, Skarbnik looked up in disbelief and exclaimed, "Well, my friend, you've beaten me fair and square! And I can't complain about that, so I'll honour my word. Come with me. I will show you where to find the best salt!"

That evening, when Szymon returned to his wife, he did a little jig in the kitchen.

"Why are you looking so pleased with yourself? Anyone would think you'd found a new vein of salt!" cried Szymonowa.

"Well I have... I did... in a way," replied her husband.

"*In a way?* What do you mean, *In a way?* Either you found it or you didn't!" said his wife.

Szymon thought of telling her about his card games with the Treasurer, but in the end decided to keep quiet. After all, did it really matter how he had found the salt? Now he would have more money – and that in itself ought to be enough to keep his wife happy. If he was playing cards and enjoying himself

at the same time, what was wrong with that?

The days passed, and Szymon's winning streak continued. And the more he won, the lazier he became. He'd sit back and enjoy an afternoon nap while Skarbnik ran around doing all the dirty work!

But one day Szymon's luck ran out. Skarbnik was getting tired of his extra work in the mine. He knew there was only one way to beat this precocious miner at cards. He'd have to put in more practice at night, in the still hours of the early morning when all the creatures of the mine were asleep.

✳ ✳ ✳

The Treasurer shuffled his cards in quiet satisfaction. He'd been through every hand, every possible combination, and now at last he knew every trick in the book. He sat back in his salt chair by the fire, puffing on his faithful pipe and dozing. Dreams of a tasty sandwich lying on the table – two pieces of freshly baked rye bread spread with a thick layer of home-churned, creamy golden butter flashed in front of his closed eyes. He could almost smell the delicious honey-coloured crust, as if his room was joined to a bakery and the warm air from the ovens was wafting through the window.

"Oh, Szymon, my lad, you do not know how much I'm looking forward to our little meeting tomorrow!" he muttered to himself.

The miner arrived at Skarbnik's card house in his usual cocksure fashion.

"Shuffle the cards, Skarbnik! Let's play!" he cried. "My colleagues can't believe how much salt I'm finding nowadays! The whole of Wieliczka is talking about me!"

Skarbnik raised an eyebrow. Arrogance was another feature he disliked and this Szymon appeared to possess it in abundance.

"Indeed, let's play, my good man. And pray to the powers above that your winning ways continue," said the Treasurer enigmatically.

Szymon scoffed. "Just deal the cards. No need to worry about praying!"

So the game began and within an hour, much to his disbelief, Szymon lost, not once, not twice – but three times! He couldn't believe it, and asked Skarbnik to play again. To his surprise, the result was the same. Now it was the Treasurer's turn to laugh.

"How does it feel to lose, and have to pay the winner his dues?" he mocked.

Szymon bit his lip. Not good. Slowly he undid his mining bag and, pulling out his second breakfast, placed a delicious-looking sandwich on the table. Skarbnik's eyes sparkled. This would be one of many, he'd make sure of that.

And so it was. Day in, day out, Szymon turned up at the card house and each time he lost, he was obliged to give Skarbnik a freshly made sandwich for his second breakfast. And now poor Szymon had to go back into the mine and look for the precious salt himself.

Every day Szymon had to make an extra sandwich. His losing streak looked as if it would never end. He reckoned he could conceal matters from his wife, but Szymonowa knew her kitchen like the skin on the back of her hand. You could ask her in the middle of the night what was in it, from the smallest cupboard to the tall pantry where they kept food, and she would always have the answer. She had noticed that her store of freshly churned butter, made with her own hands, was disappearing.

"Szymon, I only filled this butter bowl up yesterday, and it's almost empty! Do you know where it's all going?" she demanded one evening.

Szymon didn't answer. A bead of sweat trickled down his brow.

"Well, come on, where is it all going? At the rate it's disappearing, I wouldn't mind betting you're greasing the wheels of the carriages in the mine with it! And to think how much cream I use to make it!"

"Greasing… the wheels… of the carriages?" Szymon said the words slowly to himself.

"Well, I'm still waiting for an answer," she persisted. As he feared he would never see a buttered sandwich again, Szymon had no choice but to tell her how his luck had changed, and how Skarbnik was demanding a second breakfast in payment every time they played.

Szymonowa was furious.

"That greedy old Treasurer. Eating our butter! Just you let me get hold of him!"

Szymon tried to calm her down, but it was no use. His wife was a strong-willed woman.

"You've got to trick him, deceive him. Maybe you can carry an extra card up your sleeve. You've got to start winning again, Szymon. We can't afford all this butter!"

Szymon was horrified.

"Swindle the Treasurer! Are you out of your mind?"

"What's the difference? You spend most of your time hoodwinking friends. Let's face it, you've even tried to fool your wife!"

But Szymon was adamant. "Whatever I do, I will not cheat Skarbnik."

This answer did not satisfy his wife. She decided to take matters into her own hands. "There's no way I'm going to feed another mouth," she said. And from that moment onwards, Szymonowa prepared the sandwiches. When the miner was fast asleep, she crept downstairs to carry out her crafty plan. She had boiled and mashed some potatoes earlier that evening and now, using the back of a knife, she carefully spread the mixture on to a slice of bread. When the sandwich was finished, she stood back and admired her work.

"That'll teach you to eat my butter, Treasurer Skarbnik!"

✲ ✲ ✲

At their next card game, Szymon sat back on a salt chair and let Skarbnik deal the cards. The morning went badly and it wasn't long before the miner had lost twice and handed his sandwich over to the Treasurer.

"Better luck tomorrow," chuckled Skarbnik, his bushy grey eyebrows moving up and down.

A dejected Szymon stalked off swinging his pickaxe. When was he ever going to win again?

He walked through several passages thinking how much he longed for his fortune to change.

Soon he found the salt vein he'd been working on the day before, raised his pickaxe and went to strike the rock. He reeled backwards as the tool juddered against the stone, sending painful vibrations through his arms and making him drop it. He tried several times, but always the same thing happened. Before Szymon knew what was happening, he heard heavy steps along the passage and a deep angry voice boomed out: "YOU CROOK! YOU MISERABLE CROOK!"

Szymon's knees were knocking. The walls of the mine were shaking. Miners came running from all directions to see what the matter was. Skarbnik, his red cheeks puffing out, fumed over the cowering Szymon, and shoved a sandwich under the miner's nose.

"Do you think you can deceive an old man by spreading his bread with disgusting potato paste instead of butter? WELL, DO YOU?

Szymon's face turned bright red. He realised that his wife had done this. He felt a complete fool, standing there in front of the great Treasurer, with everyone looking on as Skarbnik chided him like a naughty boy...

"I... I... My wife buys her b-butter... from the market... she must have been sold a dodgy lot..." he stuttered.

"Well, tell your wife to look more closely at what she's spreading on her bread in future!" roared Skarbnik.

"I'm so sorry... It... it won't happen again," squeaked Szymon.

"You're damn sure it won't happen again, you little ragamuffin. You will leave this mine immediately and find work elsewhere. And let this be a lesson to all of you," continued the Treasurer, surveying the group of terrified miners standing with their mouths open. "Anyone who tries to cheat me will suffer the consequences!"

And with these words, he disappeared.

Poor Szymon limped back home to face his wife. He never worked below ground after that, and never found salt again – not a single grain.

Jegse and the
King of the Lakes

The fisherman looked up anxiously at a bank of sinister black clouds gathering on the horizon, and rowed faster. The shore was still a long way off. Enormous waves were flicking the weather-beaten boat backwards and forwards like fingers tossing a rubber ball. Giant drops of rain began to fall, thudding into the little vessel. Suddenly an angry wave curled itself over the man and came crashing down into the boat.

"Save me, Perkun! Don't let the lake deprive two little boys of their father!" the young sailor called out despairingly.

Thunder boomed out from the heavens and fierce lightning lit up the dark sky. Wave after wave pounded the helpless boat and pushed the man into the raging water. For just one moment he thought of his wife and two young sons, before darkness came upon him…

When the fisherman awoke, he saw blue sky above him. But he was even more surprised to see a strange man with big round eyes and green hair as slimy as seaweed leaning over him.

"Am I dreaming?" he whispered to himself, rubbing his eyes. He looked again. His boat was tied to a tree on the shore of a lake, gently bobbing on the water, and the fishing nets he'd taken out that morning were now full of fish!

"Who… who are you?" asked the fisherman, staring at the strange man and watching the sun glinting on his gold crown.

"I am Zaltis, King of the Lakes. When I realised your boat was in trouble, I came up to rescue you," said the stranger in a lilting voice.

"How… how can I ever repay you?" stuttered the fisherman.

But before he could go on, Zaltis answered, "Would you give me the most valuable thing you have? If you agree, I will make sure you always have fish for the rest of your life."

The fisherman was overjoyed. After all, there was nothing valuable he possessed that Zaltis would want. He was poor. So he agreed and, thanking the king, returned to his wife.

At the door of the meagre cottage a woman stood holding a bundle wrapped in a white cloth. She smiled, as her husband pulled back the swaddling.

"Our daughter, Jegle, was born while you were away!"

The fisherman wanted to cry out with joy and thank the heavens for such a wonderful gift. But something held him back.

"What's the matter?" asked his wife, seeing the colour drain from his cheeks.

"Nothing... she's beautiful," he replied. He could not bring himself to tell her about his strange pact with the King of the Lakes.

The years passed, and the fisherman convinced himself that it had all been a dream. Little Jegle was a beautiful girl with dark eyes and long blonde plaits. She liked nothing better than helping in the kitchen or picking blueberries in the woods.

One day, her mother fell ill and died, and Jegle took over the running of the house. While the girl kept everything in the little cottage in order, her father and brothers would be out in their boat searching for fish. Sometimes Jegle liked to walk beside the lake on her own. She would sit on a wooden bridge and dangle her feet in the cool water. There was one particular place where she would stop and watch a huge green fish swim by.

One day, coming home from the lake, Jegle unexpectedly bumped into an old woman who seemed very frail. She was a kind-hearted girl, so she invited the stranger back to the cottage for tea.

"Oh, that's very kind of you, my dear, but I am looking for the place where an old fisherman lives with his daughter Jegle."

The young girl gasped.

"I am Jegle! And this is my father's cottage," she exclaimed.

She led the woman inside and made tea.

As the mysterious woman ate her blueberry cake, her appearance began to change. Her clothes turned from drab grey rags to a dress of seaweed green.

Her voice croaked like a frog's as she spoke:

"I bring news from Zaltis, the King of the Lakes. He wants to marry you!"

Jegle laughed nervously.

"A king... wants to marry *me*? You must be mistaken!"

But the stranger insisted.

"Go to the lake tomorrow, and mark my words – you will meet your future husband!"

Like most young girls, Jegle was naturally curious, so the next day she went down to the lake and sat on her favourite bridge. She half-hoped to see her friend the fish, but instead, she saw a strange man with dark, sparkling eyes and long green hair like seaweed, standing over her.

"Where... where did you come from?" she stuttered.

"Do you remember the green fish which used to swim under your feet? Well, that fish was me. I have been in love with you for a long time, Jegle, and I wish to marry you. Once, long ago, I saved your father's life, and he agreed to give you to me in return for my help."

Jegle was astounded to hear this, but the handsome king seemed to have a strange hold on her, and she felt drawn to him.

It was only after much heartache that Jegle's father agreed to let his beloved daughter go to live with the King of the Lakes. Beneath the surface of the lake, in a sumptuous palace of shimmering silver shells, Jegle and Zaltis were married. The proud king swam with his new queen through the great kingdom of the Lakes and showered her with precious jewels.

The young girl would have been perfectly happy, except for one thing: she missed her old father...

"My dearest Zaltis, if you love me as you say you do, I beg you, let me return to the land and visit my father's cottage again," she pleaded.

Zaltis's heart sank, but he loved his wife, so he swam with Jegle to the edge of the lake and let her go up to her father's cottage in the pine woods.

The old fisherman beamed with joy when he saw her.

"Jegle! Oh Jegle! How I have missed you, my dear!"

But her brothers, seeing how happy she made their old father, determined to get their sister back from the King of the Lakes.

"Let's follow her when she goes back into the water. We'll hide in the bushes with a net, and as soon as Zaltis shows himself, we'll catch him. He won't get out alive!"

The next day, Jegle rushed down to meet her husband, while the two brothers hid in the rushes. As soon as they saw Zaltis's long green hair poking out of the water, they pounced with their net.

Jegle screamed, and ran to Zaltis.

"Leave him! Leave my husband alone! What has he ever done to you?" she called out.

But she needn't have feared. The moment that their net touched the King, the brothers turned to cold, grey stone… And there they stood, motionless, by the side of the dark lake, while Jegle ran into the water and threw her arms around her husband.

"What will my father say when he sees them like that?" she asked sadly, nodding towards the grey figures.

"Oh, don't worry, Jegle. In a few hours my spell will wear off and they can go home safely. But I doubt they will try that little trick again!"

And from that day on, beautiful Jegle and wise Zaltis lived happily together in the deep green kingdom of the Lakes.

The Turnip-Counter

There was no doubt about it, nature had not been kind to the Hunchback of Karkonosze. His spine was as crooked as a banana, his nose was a monstrous protrusion of fungal shapes, his eyes small, dark and beady, his complexion pallid, his lips thin and frugal. This ugly creature might have been redeemed by a character of inward beauty – the kind of beauty that makes spring blossoms pale in its wake. But alas, even a fading flower would have felt beautiful in the presence of this mean-spirited soul, this dry, wrinkled piece of salty seaweed. Sadly, the Hunchback of Karkonosze was as ugly inside as he was outside.

If this alone had been his lot in life, the crooked misanthrope would surely have been one of the most miserable creatures on earth. But his existence was made more bearable by his rare talent for magic. With a flick of his wand he could turn himself into one of the most handsome princes the world had ever seen.

Gone was the stooping gait and the camel-like hump. In its place stood a fine figure standing tall in black, knee-length leather boots and a gilt-studded scarlet riding-jacket. In those moments of enchantment even Karkonosze Castle, a neglected and crumbling Silesian ruin where the Hunchback had lived for more than one hundred years, stood gleaming beneath the rising sun as if it had only just been built.

The only problem with the magic was that it did not last. As it faded, the Hunchback's perfectly shaped nose slowly turned back into a mushroom-like growth, his straight back would begin to bend and bow, leaving him caught halfway between beauty and ugliness. And the hedges shielding his castle in the folds of the Silesian mountains would soon turn back into bramble bushes that kept the old ruin hidden from view. At such moments, disconsolate and world-weary, the

Hunchback of Karkonosze would retire to his turnip garden, an old field behind the castle where he grew his favourite vegetable. There he would spend hours dreaming that one day he would marry a beautiful princess. "My little treasure", he would call her.

One crisp spring morning, news came to him, whispering on the wind through blossoming branches and chirping birds, of a new treasure, one he'd never dreamed of before, so beautiful that she was almost impossible to imagine.

"Long, flowing golden hair and skin the colour of a white pearl," whispered the trees, as they rustled their branches.

"Her name is Ofka, and she is the daughter of the Piast Prince Bolko," sang the sparrows.

In the gentle babbling of a little mountain stream, the Hunchback fancied he heard her sweet, melodic voice. He saw her reflection in the shimmering haze of glacier lakes and he smelt her perfume on the breeze. It wasn't long before he was so haunted by the thought of this beautiful girl that he could not remove her image from his mind.

A day came when he could bear this unwelcome torment no longer.

"Wherever this lovely flower is, I will catch her scent and steal her delicate heart for myself!" he cried.

So he decided to search for the object of his desire – unaware that the princess had just left her castle at Swidnica for a brief stay in the Silesian mountains. Soon she was to be married to her fiancé, Prince Mieszko, a valiant, noble knight, and this was her last sojourn alone.

One day, the Hunchback was out walking when he spotted the royal entourage in the distance: two sumptuous, gold-lined carriages draped in white lace and pulled by the finest horses. As they passed by, the Hunchback concealed himself behind a clump of gorse bushes.

As he knelt there, he heard the voice of a gossipy snail: "Oh yes, they say that Princess Ofka has come to stay in the mountains with her twelve maids."

The voice which issued from the small, stripy shell made the Hunchback feel so happy, he wanted to jump in the air and shout for joy.

"By all the turnips in Karkonosze! My love is paying me a visit at last!"

Then, catching a glimpse of his reflection in a mountain lake, the full extent of his ugliness dawned on him once more.

"Fool!" he chided himself. "Step out looking like this, and she'll probably run all the way back to Swidnica!"

There was no time to lose. He rushed home, a crafty plan hatching in his mind.

✳ ✳ ✳

The following day, the Hunchback hobbled out of the castle carrying a fresh turnip under one arm. He crept through the thick forests and along the narrow leafy paths until he drew near to the place where the princess was staying. Hearing the shrill giggles of several young girls, he guessed that she was out walking with her maids.

He had his trusty wand ready in his hand. With an electrifying flash, the turnip turned into a black stallion, and the Hunchback was now wearing a smart blue-and-white military uniform. Galloping through the pine trees, he came face to face with Ofka and her retinue. She was a thousand times more beautiful in the flesh than he had ever imagined.

The princess could hardly resist looking at such a dashing man, and for a moment their eyes met.

"Have I seen you before?" she asked shyly.

The twelve maids had run off, leaving her alone with the stranger.

"I am the Prince of Karkonosze, my lady," he announced. "It appears you haven't heard about me, but I know you very well..." And he bowed in an exaggerated manner.

Before the princess could reply, he swept her up off her feet, placed her on his horse and rode briskly off into the Silesian Mountains.

"But... my maids... I can't leave them..." she sighed, as if in a trance.

"Oh don't worry. We will come back for them. I thought that you might like to see my castle," replied the handsome knight, gathering speed.

As they rode, the princess clung to her captor's blue-and-white jacket. The black horse galloped through pine forests and over mountain streams, sprays of mud splashing through the air. Its master was keen to get back to the castle before the magic wore off.

Imagine Ofka's surprise, then, when the elegant jacket she was clinging to changed into a moth-eaten rag and the prince's long, flowing brown locks turned into greasy, yellowish unkempt hair. And when he looked round at her, the prince's nose appeared to have grown a wart!

"I must be dreaming..." she whispered to herself. The words had barely left her mouth when the castle loomed up in front of them. A moment later, they stood before a crumbling ruin – and the Prince of Karkonosze had crumbled too. Gone were his charm and his good looks, and as soon as they dismounted from the horse, it changed back into a turnip!

He pulled Ofka inside the ruin. "Stay here. I'll get you some food," he barked, and ran off to turn himself back into a prince.

***

It wasn't long before Ofka began to dislike the grubby little castle and its equally shabby host, who seemed to be nothing more than a cheap conjurer.

"You give me a plate of the finest Silesian sausage, sour cabbage and dumplings, and when I go to eat it, I find nothing but a bowl of lumpy gravy!"

"My dearest, you are so ungrateful!" he huffed.

"Ungrateful! I didn't ask to be fed by a hunchback. You're not a *real* prince and this isn't a *real* castle. But I am a real princess, engaged to be married to Mieszko, who is a real knight. I insist you let me go at once!"

The Hunchback sneered.

"I will never let you go, my dear, until you promise me that you will be my wife."

"That's impossible. I'm in love with another man!" she answered.

"But I've given you everything. You even have your maids here with you."

"Maids! These aren't my maids. Just look at them! They're just a pile of stinking turnips!"

It was true. When the princess had complained of loneliness, the Hunchback had brought her twelve turnips. "Touch these with my wand, and you will have your maids back again," he had told her. But they had proved to be no more than shadows, and as she watched, the skin on their faces had begun to wrinkle and one by one, their bodies started to shrink and get rounder!

"See!" she wailed. "Nothing but old turnips!"

The Hunchback stormed out, slamming the door behind him.

"It's quite simple. Marry me, and I'll let you out," he called back to her.

Alone in her room with its shabby, damp walls and dingy windows, the princess began to weep bitter tears.

"Oh dearest Mieszko. If only you knew where I was and could come and rescue me. How am I going to get out of here?"

If only she had known it, a little sparrow perched on the window ledge heard her plea, and flew off to tell Prince Mieszko of her plight.

* * *

All night the princess sat up and thought. Somehow she must trick this horrible imposter and escape. And by morning she had a plan.

When the Hunchback knocked on her door with a breakfast of eggs and bread in one hand, the princess thanked him and said, "I have something important to tell you." Imagine the Hunchback's surprise and delight when the princess declared: "I have decided to marry you…"

The crooked old misanthrope clapped his hands and dropped down on one knobbly knee. But before he could speak, Ofka added, "on condition that we have the most enormous wedding ever seen in the Silesian mountains. I want to invite everyone – all my friends, my family, my servants – everyone!"

The Hunchback was speechless. He couldn't believe his luck.

"Now," continued Ofka, "go out into your garden and count exactly how many turnips you have. That is the number of guests I will invite."

The master of Karkonosze castle was delighted. What a splendid idea! "Good Lord!" he cried. "We'll have a feast! Do you know how many turnips I've got in that garden? Hundreds, thousands… dare I say it, millions! I've been growing the damn things all my life!"

And with that, he skipped joyously out to the field, and bending down, began to count the rows and rows of turnips.

As soon as he had gone, the clever princess waved the magic wand over one of the turnip-maids, uttered a little spell which the Hunchback had taught her – and was soon riding away from the castle on a white mare. Free – at last!

Her horse was just about to become a turnip again, when she spotted a familiar figure in the distance. It was her beloved fiancé, Prince Mieszko, who had left his home at Raciborz and was out searching for his sweetheart!

So delighted were they to see each other again,

the princess hardly had time to tell her story before the prince said to her, "My poor dear, you look exhausted! Quick, let's ride at once to my father's castle. We can be married in a few days." And he smiled at the thought of this beautiful, clever woman who had outwitted her captor, and thanked the heavens for sending the little sparrow to him.

As for the Hunchback of Karkonosze, he is still in his turnip garden trying to come up with the right number of guests for his wedding. The creatures of Karkonosze can't stop laughing at him, and they sing, "*Liczyrzepa, Liczyrzepa*… look at old *Liczyrzepa*!" which, as you have probably guessed, means "Turnip-counter".

But all this chanting only makes the Hunchback cross, and he shakes his knotty little fists at the sky before starting all over again.

Well, counting turnips is not an easy task, you know. They all look the same!

The Copper Coin
of Wineta

Beyond the white sandy beaches of the Baltic coast, in the depths of the countryside, a prosperous couple lived on their estate. They had everything they wished for – except a child. How many times had Ewelina, the landowner's wife, lain awake at night longing for the next day to bring her a son or daughter to hold?

"Wieslaw, my dearest, I can't sleep... Wieslaw! Are you awake?"

Her husband would turn over, trying to hide his irritation at being woken, and reply sleepily, "Yes, dear... I am now..."

"There are so many orphans in the world. Surely we could find one and bring it up as our own child..."

"But where shall we find a child with a good heart?

We'd probably have to travel the length and breadth of the country," lamented her husband.

"Well, let's see what the new day brings," replied Ewelina, and with hope glimmering in her heart she would fall asleep and dream about a young boy who was rescuing her from great danger…

***

A sudden commotion woke Ewelina. She sat up in bed and saw a red light through the curtain of her bedroom window. Someone was shrieking in the yard below, "Wake up! Wake up! Fire! Fire!"

At first Ewelina thought she was still dreaming, but when the frantic voice continued, she shook her husband violently.

Old Wieslaw jumped out of bed like a hare and raced downstairs to find a hose. Outside, a young boy was shouting and desperately trying to douse the flames with buckets of water. "Quick, get out of the house! Smother the flames before they spread!"

And by the time Ewelina came down, the two of them had put out the fire.

Wieslaw was puzzled. Who was this young boy who had saved their lives, and where had he come from? He asked the boy, who replied, "My mother

and father died a long time ago. I'm travelling around in search of a job…"

"So you are an orphan!" Ewelina put her hands together and looked up to the skies with gratitude, then at her husband.

"From this day onwards you will stay with us. It's the least we can do for you, since you have saved our lives!" she exclaimed.

Young Slawek, for that was his name, was soon comfortably settled with his foster parents. He was a hard worker and it wasn't long before the estate had recovered from the fire. The harvest was bountiful, the animals were breeding, the labourers were healthy and every day, merchants travelled from far and wide to buy the fresh vegetables, mellow oats, ripe wheat and creamy milk produced on the bustling farm.

It was while listening to the merchants that Slawek heard tales of the mysterious town of Wineta where, they said, the coloured houses touched the blue sky and the streets were full of busy stalls teemingwith the riches of the world: nutmeg, cloves and pepper from the Spice Islands, tea from China, mangoes and pomegranates from Malaya, coffee from Brazil… Slawek's mouth watered at the thought of these exotic foods. And that wasn't all. He also heard tales of sparkling diamonds and blood-red rubies as big as eggs!

Slawek made up his mind: he would go and see Wineta for himself!

✳ ✳ ✳

Old Ewelina looked fondly at her foster son as she prepared him a generous bundle of food.

"Slawek, you know how sorry your father and I are that you're leaving us. You will come back soon, won't you?"

The boy's big blue eyes were sparkling at the prospect of the adventure to come, but he loved his foster parents and the thought of leaving them filled him with sadness.

"If it hadn't been for you, my lad, this farm would have burnt to a cinder. We need you here all the time…" added his foster father, and his voice shook as he spoke.

✳ ✳ ✳

Heavy rain followed the boy all the way to the coast. Three long days of blustery squalls and showers sent him and his trusty horse diving for the cover of woodland and forest. But when he arrived at his longed-for destination, golden sun shone down on the pretty little coastal town of Wineta with its coloured houses, cobbled square and cloth-covered market stalls. Slawek was astonished. He had never seen such a beautiful place in his life. He quickly dismounted and left his horse with the stable boy at a local inn, then made his way back into the square to see what the merchants had to sell.

While the young traveller was admiring the hustle and bustle of the market, he trod on something hard. Underneath his sandal was a small copper coin. Slawek bent down to pick it up. He rolled it in his hand and read the inscription: *Grosz pomorski* ("Pomeranian penny").

It was hardly worth anything, and in such a wealthy town he imagined few would notice it. But being an honest, hard-working boy, Slawek wanted to trace its owner and give the coin back.

The moment he called out, "Does this coin belong to anybody?" people started crowding in upon him. The greedy faces of strangers leered into his face.

"That's my coin."

"It belongs to me..."

"No, it doesn't! It's mine. Give it to me..."

"Thief!"

One loud voice boomed out above all the rest. Slawek looked up into the red face of the market guard.

"Boy! Did you find this coin or did you steal it? Answer me!" he bellowed.

"I found it, sir. I was just trying…"

"Liar!" roared the guard. "That coin is mine. You stole it! To the tower with you!"

Inside the tower, poor Slawek tossed and turned on the cold stone floor. Hundreds of thoughts went through his mind as he tried to make sense of what had happened. Had he done something wrong? He had stumbled on a coin and tried to find the owner, and now he was accused of stealing it!

The moon shone through a small window in the stone wall and strange shadows played tricks on his mind. Slawek woke in a cold sweat. Horrible faces crowded in upon him. In desperation, the boy called out, "Mother, father, help me! You were right… why did I ever leave you?"

Early the next morning when the cockerel had crowed, the grumpy jailer opened the tower doors and dragged his dishevelled prisoner before the Mayor of Wineta. This short, fat man with dark beady eyes had the look of a man who enjoyed his food and nourished himself on daily lies. Slawek was just reflecting on this, when the plump Mayor turned on his heels, tapped his pointy black boots together and cried, "What is the meaning of this? I dropped a coin here... in this very square, yesterday... and you... ragamuffin... you crook... have stolen it!"

The Mayor's fat cheeks were bright purple. Everyone stared at him, but no one dared speak. All the merchants of Wineta knew that the Mayor had been out of town on business the previous day, so how could he have dropped a coin in the square?

Slawek tried to defend himself.

"Sir, please... forgive me. I only picked the coin up. I had every intention of returning it... to its rightful owner."

"Seven years you will get for this! Seven long years in jail!" roared the furious Mayor.

These words had hardly left his mouth when all at once the clear blue sky turned pitch-black and bright yellow bolts of lightning forked towards the earth. A few seconds later, thunder boomed out

angrily, making the ground shake and shudder.

Slawek stood petrified, his fists clasped tight. As he watched, he couldn't believe his eyes... All around him the beautiful town was sinking into the deep blue sea. Houses and old buildings toppled and crumbled, and the powdery dust fell into the boiling water and was greedily devoured by the frothy waves.

The boy closed his eyes and thought of his beloved parents...

When he dared to open his eyes once more, he was standing alone on a white sandy beach, his left hand clasping the copper coin. There was no sign of the town of Wineta. Everything had gone: the clipper ships, the busy harbour, the flamboyant buildings, the marble lighthouse.

Slawek lifted his arm and flung the coin out into the sea. Terrible greed had driven these people mad. Now he wanted nothing to do with the money.

Relief flooded through him. Feeling light and hopeful, he turned quickly and made his way home. He longed to be back with his dear parents, working hard on their farm.

Never again did Slawek return to the coast. But one

hundred years later, a young sailor claimed he had seen the mirage of a ghost town while out fishing in the Baltic Sea. He spoke of a giant harbour and colourful stalls with rich produce laid out in the crowded town square, a place where everyone seemed intent on just one thing – money.

King Fish

In the murky depths of Lake Sniardwy, the water was pitch black and clouds of sand and mud swirled around the tendrils of luminous green weeds growing beside a castle of rocks. All the little fish knew the castle.

Sum the cat-fish twitched his wiry moustache as he stood on his tail before this underwater fortress, waiting to be summoned inside. The stone drawbridge was down, the coral portcullis up and the pink anemone was flying from the tower. King Fish was at home, and the catfish imagined the monarch with huge fins, perched upon his throne, a crown of coral upon his head.

And Sum thought, "How does my own little moustache compare with His Majesty's magnificent grey whiskers? Who am I to tell the king about that strange *thing* that has appeared on the far side of the lake? It's probably nothing – and then, just think how angry he'll be if I've disturbed his afternoon rest! But what if it turns out to be *something*, and I haven't told him? Just imagine how angry he'll be then... and what will happen to me?"

The gloomy dungeons beneath the castle were rumoured to contain the bones of many unfortunate fishermen who had trespassed into these waters, and Sum imagined there was plenty more room where a troublesome little fish could be locked away.

"There is a cat-fish to see you, my Lord."

Sum's bristly whiskers twitched nervously as he was ushered in.

"What is it, my little chap? Speak up," bellowed King Fish.

"Your Majesty, on the far side of the lake a huge iron monster has invaded the water. None of us knows what it is."

King Fish opened one eye wider than the other.

"A monster? In my lake? We'll see about that!" And with an angry flap of his fins which sent bubbles coursing through the castle corridors, the great white fish, big as a shark, burst out through the portcullis and into the open water.

Tribes of little creatures who lived in the lake followed, singing cautionary songs that warned the king to take care. But King Fish was angry, and he swam right up to the monster – straight into the heavy iron net which the fishermen had laid to trap him.

CLANG! went the giant bars, as the locks snapped shut. King Fish roared and thrashed around wildly, but the metal was too strong for him and all he did was move the net closer to the shore.

"Hey, look! We've got a catch!" shouted the excited fishermen on the bank.

It took twelve strong men to hoist the enormous fish in and they gasped as they hauled him ashore.

"Wow! Have you ever seen such a monster? Just look at the size of his whiskers!"

King Fish thrashed around as they hauled him on to a cart and wheeled him to the courtroom. They sat him in the dock before three wizened judges with grey wigs and powdered faces.

One by one they read out accusations.

"You stand accused of disturbing fishing in this lake! And by doing so, you are making people hungry. Don't you know that fish is like bread?" declared the first judge.

"You are also accused of wilfully damaging nets and boats belonging to the fishermen, thus allowing their catch to escape," said the second judge. He added, "And here in this idyllic land of lakes and forests, we can do without a monster like you disturbing the peace!"

"Lastly, you are accused of coveting things which belong to everyone," declared the third judge.

King Fish stared defiantly at his accusers, and with hardly a twitch of his long, grey whiskers, he replied:

"Let me put this to you three judges. Why is it that my fish, those whom I guard within this lake, never trespass into fishermen's territory – and yet these pirates have brought their boats, nets and rods into our waters without stopping to consider that the lake does not belong to them."

The judges turned purple when they heard this, and decided to punish the monstrous fish once and for all.

Together they cried, "For showing such contempt, you shall die a horrible death!"

King Fish did not move.

"Go on, then. Kill me! But remember all the followers I have in this lake. When word gets round that you have murdered me in cold blood, your supper might not be so easy to catch. Kill me, and see how quickly famine spreads throughout your land."

The judges whispered among themselves, "This King Fish is no fool. It might be better to change the sentence without, of course, making it any more lenient…"

They turned once more to the prisoner.

"Very well," they cried. "You shall keep your life, but we will tie you to the bridge with an iron chain for the rest of your life. When you die of natural causes, a wooden fish will be chained to the bridge in your place. Let the world remember that you cannot make the fish in this lake rebel against us."

So they carried the giant creature back to the lake on a rusty cart, lashed a chain around him and secured it to the bridge.

As King Fish was chained up, he declared, "This chain shall remain to remind the world how you seek to impose your will upon it!"

And with these words, he slipped out of the chain and disappeared beneath the surface of the lake.

Nobody ever saw him again.

Water of Life

Maciek laid a soft rag soaked in cool water on his mother's forehead. His hands trembled and he felt tears welling up in his eyes, for he had already tried many different herbs and prepared all kinds of tinctures, infusions and tonics – but all in vain. His mother showed no sign of improvement.

Gently closing the door of their wooden cottage behind him, he walked towards the ancient forest and followed the winding mountain stream to the old healer's hut. Most people kept away from the place – but Maciek was desperate...

"You've tried all the usual herbs, you say? What – even columbine and plantain? And nothing happens? No improvement? Well, my lad, there is only one thing left..." The wrinkled crone wheezed, her voice creaky like a jackdaw.

Maciek stared at her hopefully.

"Whatever it is, I need to know. I'll do anything...

anything at all, only help me," he pleaded.

The old woman lowered her voice as if she didn't want the creatures of the forest to hear…

"Far away from here is a huge mountain called Sobotka. On its summit you will find a talking tree and a miraculous spring bursting out of the ground. It's the water of life. This is the only thing which can help your poor mother. It brings back health and is reputed to…" – the old woman paused, drew a breath, leaned closer to the young boy and then whispered eagerly in his ear – "bring the dead to life again!"

She went on, "Reputed, because no one has ever found it. The mountain lies beyond three dark forests and three deep rivers…"

Maciek's eyes sparkled with hope.

"I will go immediately, if it can save my dear mother's life!"

"Ah, my boy, it is not so easy. Many have set out with the same thought, and never returned. You can't imagine how many foul monsters and wicked temptations are hiding along the way. Fall prey to any of them, and you will be turned to stone," warned the old woman.

Young Maciek thought again of his poor mother confined so pitifully to her sick bed. Nothing would stop him from finding the mountain and spring. He thanked the old healer and ran home like the wind.

He tried to feed his mother a small bowl of vegetable broth. Then, promising he would not be gone long, he picked up a wooden stick, wrapped a few provisions in a yellow scarf and tied his bundle to the end.

Maciek kept the image of his mother at the front of his mind as he walked beneath the towering firs, giant oaks and slender beeches. He crossed three deep rivers on flimsy rafts and seemed to see his mother's face in the bubbling water of the mountain streams.

One morning, when the dew was still fresh upon the ground, the boy left the last forest and found himself staring up at the most sinister mountain he'd ever seen – Mount Sobotka. Its rugged sides were covered with trees clustered together in tufts, like knotted hair sprouting from a giant head. Maciek couldn't see the summit, but he knew he had to reach the top fast. He began his ascent up a narrow winding path.

He hadn't gone far, when he heard the hiss of snakes. He froze on the spot as he saw several vipers in the dense undergrowth poking long pink tongues out of their brown-and-green-mottled heads. For an instant he wanted to turn back, but the thought of his poor mother spurred him on. He closed his eyes tightly and passed unhurt through the venomous snakes' den.

The gnarled trees grew closer together in this part of the wood, and the narrow path wound steeply over gravel and loose boulders. All at once Maciek slipped, losing his footing and almost crashing to the ground. "Surely", he whispered to himself, "there must be an easier way up than this." And as he spoke, strange voices started to plague him. Haunting words sailed in on the wind, squeezing their way through the jungle of firs and pines.

"Why labour up such a difficult path, Maciek?"

"Turn round. Behind you is an easier way…"

Maciek cupped his hands over his ears…

"Look at the wide path on your left. It's easier. Follow it, follow it…"

But no temptation could win the boy over. He ignored the voices and kept walking along the same track. And as he ventured deeper into the dark forest, a terrible fear overcame him. A hungry wolf howled, a piercing cry that made the hairs on the back of his neck stick up. At times it was so gloomy, it felt like night, but the thought of his mother led Maciek on towards the light.

A second wolf howled. The dark forest was suddenly lit up, and out of a tree hung a dozen goggling imps with horns. Dread gripped Maciek. He wanted to turn back and run, but the frail voice of his mother pleaded with him to carry on.

"My dear son, you are my only hope! If you turn back, I will surely die…"

All at once Maciek felt hot air on his face, like a gust of tropical wind. Surely, the higher he climbed, the cooler it should be. With a dry mouth and stinging eyes he wrestled his way onwards in the sweltering heat.

A flicker of red danced in the distance. Maciek shouted, "FIRE!"

Yellow, orange and red flames were spreading across the whole mountainside. But still Macick struggled on. And to his surprise, he noticed that despite the fire, the flames did not touch him.

It wasn't long before he spotted a vast limestone cave. Inside, a huge yellow and green beast lay sleeping, smoke trailing from its nostrils. A dragon! Maciek felt a sudden pain in his legs. Looking down, he saw hundreds of lizard-like creatures with tiny razor teeth snapping at his ankles. He clenched his teeth, brushed the monsters off and kept walking. Nothing was going to stop him reaching the top now.

But just as he thought the worst was over, an enormous crash sent him diving for cover. A great boulder was rolling down through the dark forest flattening the trees on its path to the bottom of the mountain. Maciek thanked the skies he wasn't down there.

He was nearing the top. All he had to do now was get through the gully ahead.

Out of nowhere, a well-dressed man in a gold hat stepped into his path, his teeth glinting in a sneer. He thrust a leather bag into Maciek's path.

"Here, take these gold coins, and go. Leave this mountain now, and you can go home a rich man…"

For a moment Maciek hesitated, thinking of all the wonderful things he could buy for himself. But would a bag of coins buy his mother's health? Waving the man away, he walked firmly forward, only to bump into a blue-eyed, fair-haired young girl so beautiful that he couldn't help stopping to gaze at her.

"Come with me! Forget all your troubles. We will run away together and be happy…"

Maciek felt a strong desire to take her hand. Oh, how he longed to escape with this beautiful woman! But deep inside, he knew he only had one mother and he could not abandon her, having come so far. He closed his eyes and grimly walked on.

When he looked up again, he saw the elusive mountain peak above him. Only a tiny stream strewn with pebbles and boulders lay between young Maciek and his goal. He set foot on a rock – and reeled backwards, for as he touched it, water began to seep out.

"Help me, Maciek!" cried a voice.

As he crossed, placing his feet carefully on one rock and then another, the voice was joined by a chorus of weeping and wailing.

"So long have we lain here, turned to stone for our weakness. Please help us!"

But Maciek wouldn't stop.

I will remember you on my way down. I promise," he called back.

With one last push, the boy heaved himself up on to the mountain peak. But it wasn't the view of the dazzling forest below, or the snowy white clouds in the sky which caught the young man's attention. He was too busy staring at the lone fir tree in the midst of the peak, and the great white-and-grey hawk that perched in its branches. Underneath, in a narrow cleft, Maciek saw a tiny mountain spring from which water as pure as the sky flowed. All around the thick base of the lonely fir and scattered over the summit lay

hundreds of boulders similar to those Maciek had passed on his way up. The young man stared in wonder as the enormous hawk stretched out its wings and flew up into the blue sky beyond the clouds.

"This is it! This is what I've come for!" he cried, but his words were interrupted. The great bird had flown back to the tree carrying a golden jug in its claws.

The fir tree began to move its crooked branches. Maciek stared in wonder as a strange voice boomed out.

"I can see you've never heard a tree talk, my boy. Well, believe me, we do occasionally, when we have something important to say. Now, you look at that jug which my friend is holding. Take it, and fill it with water from this spring. Dip a branch in the water, then go home and sprinkle it on your mother's forehead."

Nervously, Maciek took the heavy jug from the hawk and did exactly as the tree had said. As he filled the golden vessel to the rim, he accidentally spilt a little of the water on some of the rocks. Imagine his surprise when they began to change into human beings, and proceeded to follow him down the steep mountain. Crowds of poor folk who had been turned to stone for giving in to temptation and fear on their way to the mountain peak, were now freed – and all this, thanks to one brave boy!

✳ ✳ ✳

Maciek's journey back through the dark forests and across the deep rivers didn't seem as long as before. When he arrived at his mother's cottage, he stood outside and called out, "Mother! Mother! It's your son, Maciek. I'm back!"

But there was no answer.

He pushed open the door, trying not to spill the precious water, and found his mother lying motionless on the bed. Was he too late?

"I did it, mother. I brought this back for you,"

he cried. And he sprinkled a few drops of water on her face.

For some time he sat with his head in his hands.

All at once, he heard a voice say weakly, "Have I been asleep long, my son?"

Words cannot describe young Maciek's joy. From then on, he knew what real happiness was – and if he hadn't travelled so far, he would never have found it.

About the stories

My wife Malgosia and her mother, Joanna Hoscilowicz, have told me many Polish stories, including those in this collection. I have also referred to the following:

The Turnip-Counter
W Gorach Olbrzymich
Stanislaw Belza (1849-1929)
(published Krakow, Gebethner i Wolff, 1898)
The Karkonosze Mountains are the highest in the Sudeten Chain, criss-crossed by winding footpaths. The upper parts are a national park, recognised by UNESCO as a World Biosphere Reserve.

The Mermaid of Warsaw
Syrena
Artur Oppman (1867-1931)
Today the mermaid is a symbol of Warsaw, appearing on postcards, flags and many other souvenirs in the craft shops of the city.

Skarbnik's Second Breakfast

Legendy i Basnie Slaskie,

Stanislaw Wasylewski (1885-1953)

(published Slask, Katowice, 1957)

Visit the Wieliczka Salt Mine at www.kopalnia.pl

Jegle and the King of the Lakes

Litwa, Dziela wszystkie, t.53,

Henryk Oskar Kolberg (1814-90)

(published Ossolineum, Wroclaw, 1966)

The Copper Coin of Wineta

Legenda Winety: Studium historyczne

Ryszard Kiersnowski (1926-2006)

(published Ossolineum, Krakow, 1950)

Chronicles of Adam of Bremen, circa 1075

The Goats of Poznan

Oral tradition

Visit the Poznan History Museum in the Town Hall at www.mnp.art.pl/oddzialy/ratusz

The goats you see today butting their heads beneath the clock face are not the original ones carved by Pietrek. Those were destroyed around 1551 by a violent thunderbolt.

King Fish
Wspomnienia Polesia, Wolynia i Litwy
Jozef Ignacy Kraszewski (1812-87)
(published Wilno, 1840)

Water of Life
Basn o Sobotniej Gorze
Roman Zamorski (1822-1961)
(published 1852)

Richard Monte is a children's book reviewer.
He also works as a children's bookseller for Waterstone's.
His first novel for children, *The Flood Tales*, was
published by Pavilion Books in 2000. He has travelled
extensively in Poland, not only to the major cities
but also on the Baltic Coast and in the Tatra Mountain
region, and he has contributed articles on Poland to
the BBC History Magazine and History Today.
Reviewers described his first Frances Lincoln collection
of Polish legends, *The Dragon of Krakow*, as
'brimming with humour, magic and visual charm...
a delight for all ages'. Richard lives in St Albans,
Hertfordshire with his Polish wife and two children.

www.richardmonte.co.uk

THE DRAGON OF KRAKOW
Richard Monte
Illustrated by Paul Hess

These Polish folk tales have a delightfully mischievous character all their own. To create his sparkling collection, Richard Monte has gathered some of Poland's favourite stories from all over the country: *The Golden Duck* hails from Warsaw, *The King Who Was Eaten by Mice* comes from Gniezno, *The Gingerbread Bees* is from Torun, while *The Dragon of Krakow* tells the legendary story of King Krak and how his beautiful city came to be built. Brimming with humour, magic and Paul Hess's exuberant illustrations, these retellings uncover a fascinating land and people.

"Brimming with humour, magic and visual charm, Richard Monte's retellings are a delight for all ages." *Betty Bookmark*

"A perfect introduction to another country's heritage." *School Librarian*

"Sparkling retellings." *Scholastic Best Books of 2008*

**A FISTFUL OF PEARLS
AND OTHER STORIES FROM IRAQ**
Elizabeth Laird
Illustrated by Shelley Fowles

Having lived in Iraq, award-winning novelist Elizabeth Laird
has gathered together a wealth of folk stories spiced with
humour, lighthearted trickery and the rose-scented
enchantment of the Arabian Nights. Here are nine of the best –
stories of boastful tailors, mean-spirited misers, magical quests
and a handful of lively animal tales – meticulously researched,
elegantly retold and playfully illustrated by Shelley Fowles
to reveal the true, traditional heart of Iraq.

"Enchanting. Its baddies are wolves and thieves;
its stories are fabulous." *The Daily Telegraph*

**THE PRINCE WHO THOUGHT HE WAS A ROOSTER
AND OTHER JEWISH STORIES**
Ann Jungman
Illustrated by Sarah Adams
Introduced by Michael Rosen

A Chilli Champion?… a Golem?… a Prince who thinks
he's a Rooster? Find them all in this collection of traditional
Jewish tales – lovingly treasured, retold and carried through
countries as far apart as Poland, Tunisia, Czechoslovakia,
Morocco, Russia and Germany, with a cast of eccentric princes,
flustered tailors, wise rabbis and the oldest champion of all!
Seasoned with wit, humour and magic, Ann Jungman's
retellings of stories familiar to Jewish readers are sure
to delight a new, wider readership.

'Timeless fables of derring-do.'
Irish Examiner

GHADDAR THE GHOUL
AND OTHER PALESTINIAN STORIES
Sonia Nimr
Illustrated by Hannah Shaw
Introduced by Ghada Karmi

Why do Snakes eat Frogs?
What makes a Ghoul turn Vegetarian?
How can a Woman make a Bored Prince Smile?
The answers to these and many other questions can be
found in this delicious anthology of Palestinian folk stories.
A wry sense of humour runs through their cast of
characterful women, genial tricksters and mischievous animals.
Sonia Nimr's upbeat storytelling, bubbling with wit and humour,
will delight readers discovering for the first time
the rich tradition of Palestinian storytelling.

"A must in any self-respecting school library shelves."
School Librarian